www.booksbyboxer.com

Bee Three Publishing is an imprint of Books By Boxer
Published by
Books By Boxer, Leeds, LS13 4BS, UK
Books by Boxer (EU), Dublin, D02 P593, IRELAND
Boxer Gifts LLC, 955 Sawtooth Oak Cir, VA 22802, USA
© Books By Boxer 2025
cs@boxer.gifts
All Rights Reserved
MADE IN CHINA
ISBN: 9781915410863

BEGINNING

Since the beginning of time, people have been pulling pranks on each other and joking about current affairs. Some jokes have made it to the 21st century, whereas others have (gladly) been left in the far far past!
Here are just SOME of history's first, worst, and funniest jokes!

THE OLDEST JOKE EVER

The oldest ever joke was found on an ancient Sumerian tablet, from around 4500-1900 BC. It's also a 'walked into the bar' joke!

The humor is lost on us these days, but some experts think that the dog in question was a guard dog. So when he guards the tavern (or rather, a brothel), walks in and then opens the door so he can see, the dog in fact exposes the customers inside. That's one theory, at least!

A DOG WALKED INTO A TAVERN
AND SAID, 'I CAN'T SEE A THING.
I'LL OPEN THIS ONE.'

TOILET HUMOR

Something that will never get old, even our ancient ancestors had a soft spot for cheeky fart jokes! This joke came from Mesopotamia, now know as Southern Iraq - in the form of fatherly advice from father to son!

SOMETHING WHICH HAS NEVER OCCURRED SINCE TIME IMMEMORIAL: A YOUNG WOMAN DID NOT FART IN HER HUSBAND'S LAP.

ROYAL BANTER

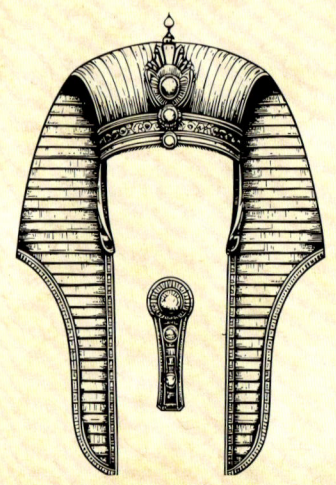

While making your monarch the butt of the joke might not be wise, it sure makes for some good comedy! Rumored to be about the Ancient Egyptian King Snofru, the joke was found in the Westcar Papyrus (and is now displayed in the Egyptian Museum of Berlin!)

How do you entertain a bored pharaoh? You sail a boatload of young women dressed only in fishing nets down the Nile and urge the pharaoh to go catch a fish.

JOKING EGYPTIANS

Who said royalty can't dish out their own jokes? The Ancient Egyptian King Djehutymes was a bit of a jester, and wrote this rib-tickler in one of his many letters!

A woman who was blind in one eye has been married to a man for 20 years. When he found another woman he said to her, "I shall divorce you because you are said to be blind in one eye." And she answered him: "Have you just discovered that after 20 years of marriage!?"

ANCIENT DAD JOKES

Who'd have thought dad jokes would have been popular in ancient Greece? This pretty terrible joke is sure to make a few ancient teens groan with embarrassment!

Odysseus tells the Cyclops that his real name is nobody. When Odysseus instructs his men to attack the Cyclops, the Cyclops shouts: "Help, Nobody is attacking me!" No one comes to help.

THE OLDEST 'YOUR MOTHER JOKE'

Ever heard or told a 'Your Mother' joke?
Of course you have.

Well, it turns out that people have been
telling these jokes since at least the
Roman Empire! Historians unearthed this
ancient joke:

The Emperor Augustus was touring the Empire when he noticed a man in the crowd who bore a striking resemblance to himself.

Intrigued, he asked: 'Was your mother at one time in service at the palace?'. 'No, your highness,' the man replied, 'but my father was.'

CICERO CHUCKLES

Quoted by the Roman statesman
Cicero, his works greatly influenced
the Latin language, and they bring us
laughs even today!

A VERY SHORT WITNESS AT A TRIAL COMES UP TO THE STAND. "MIND IF I ASK YOU SOMETHING?" SAYS PHILIPPUS. "KEEP IT SHORT," SNAPS THE JUDGE. "NO PROBLEM," HE REPLIES,

"I JUST HAVE A TINY BIT TO ASK."

CICERO CHUCKLES

"I'LL COME HAVE DINNER AT YOUR HOUSE,"
A MAN TELLS THIS ONE-EYED FRIEND OF
MINE,

"I SEE YOU'VE GOT A PLACE FOR ONE."

There was a candidate running for office whose father was believed to be a cook. When he went to ask a man for his vote, Cicero, who was standing by, piped up,

"Roast assured — I'll support you!"

CICERO CHUCKLES

IN THE FINALE OF A SPEECH, A MAN THOUGHT HE'D MOVED HIS AUDIENCE TO PITY. ONCE HE SAT DOWN, HE ASKED CATULUS, "DO YOU THINK I MOVED THEM TO PITY?" "OH HELL YEAH," REPLIED CATULUS,

"I DON'T THINK ANYONE'S SO HARD-HEARTED THAT THEY DIDN'T FIND YOUR SPEECH PITIFUL."

CICERO CHUCKLES

Elagabalus, emperor of Rome, loved wild animals, and had many tamed tigers and leopards, among others. To prank his friends who visited, he would have his large cats jump onto couches beside the guests, and would also lead them to the rooms of passed-out drunk friends to give them a fright!

Not only this, he may be the founding father of the Whoopie Cushion! Elagabalus liked to prank his guests at the dinner table by placing cushions that let out farting noises when sat upon!

THE OLDEST PRINTED JOKE BOOK

The world's oldest ever joke book comes from Ancient Greece in 300-400 AD. Written by Hierocles and Philagrius, the book, Philogelos (or Laughter-Lover), still inspires jokes to this day!

Asked by the court barber how he wanted his hair cut, the King replied: "In silence."

'Wishing to teach his donkey not to eat, a pedant did not offer him any food. When the donkey died of hunger he said: 'I've had a great loss! Just when he had learned not to eat, he died.'

THE OLDEST PRINTED JOKE BOOK

A student dunce went swimming and almost drowned. So now he swears he'll never get into water until he's really learned to swim.

STEAMING AT THE EARS

Anthemius of Tralles, a Greek architect from the 5th century knew his stuff when it came to building, so when he and his neighbor got into a heated argument, he did what any handyman would and connected his boilers to his neighbors cellar using a hose. When lit, the steam produced by the boilers would shoot out with such force that his neighbor thought there was an earthquake!

To prank his monastry, 15th century monk Thomas Betson hollowed out an apple and placed a beetle inside so it would rock back on forth on its own. He was also known for his levitating tricks, where he would use hair and a drip of wax to make eggs float in the air!

MEDIEVAL MISCHIEF

The Medieval Italian scholar Poggio Bracciolini was viewed as one of the brightest men of his time, and he just so happened to collect jokes about Italian people of all classes...

One of our fellow citizens, an intimate friend of mine, is extremely thin and lean. Someone was wondering what be the reason for this. Another friend answered: "It is the plainest thing of the world, the man sits an hour when taking his food, and two hours, when ejecting it."

The wife, observing a ram copulating with a sheep, asks how the ram chooses his mate, to which the husband answers that the ram chooses the sheep that farts. He confirms to her that humans work the same way, after which she farts, and they have sex; she farts again, with the same result. When she farts a third time, the husband says, "I'm not making love to you again, even if you s**t out your soul.

In the late 1200s, Robert II (Count of Artois) found himself a bit of a prankster. He owned a castle, and wanted to make it as entertaining as possible! He would often use a secret trapdoor on others, and set boobytraps - opening a window would cause water to squirt at you, browsing books would cause you to have soot flinged into your face, and looking through the mirror would inevitably cause you to be covered in flour!

TUDOR TICKLERS

In a time most noted for beheadings and divorces, one might think there would be no time for cracking one-liners... But you'd be wrong!

The tudors prided themselves on their quick-witted humor, and their jokes can still raise a laugh today!

WHY DOTH A COW LIE DOWN?
BECAUSE IT CANNOT SIT.

WHAT BEAST IS IT THAT HATH HER
TAIL BETWEEN HER EYES?

IT IS A CAT WHEN SHE LICKETH HER
A**E.

How many calves' tails would it take to reach from the earth to the sky?

No more than one, if it be long enough.

WHY DO MEN MAKE AN OVEN IN A
TOWN?

BECAUSE THEY CANNOT MAKE A TOWN
IN AN OVEN.

WHICH ARE THE MOST PROFITABLE
SAINTS OF THE CHURCH?

THOSE PAINTED ON THE GLASS
WINDOWS, FOR THEY KEEP THE WIND
FROM WASTING THE CANDLES.

WHAT A JOKE!
FACTS

The word 'joke' originates from the late 17th century (1670 in fact!), and is actually derived from the Latin word 'Jocus'!

THE FIRST EVER 'KNOCK KNOCK' JOKE

Most experts believe the first knock, knock joke was created by none other than... Shakespeare! Found in Macbeth, a man knocks at Macbeth's door, in which he replies "Who's there?"

It didn't become a widely used joke until much later, in 1936!

FEVER FOR FUN

Famous astrologer John Partridge sold bogus predictions within his almanacs to the public. In 1708, he predicted that London would be hit with a fever in April.

To humour him, Jonathan Swift decided to play a prank on John, and published his own almanac under a fake name, claiming that John would die from the very same fever.

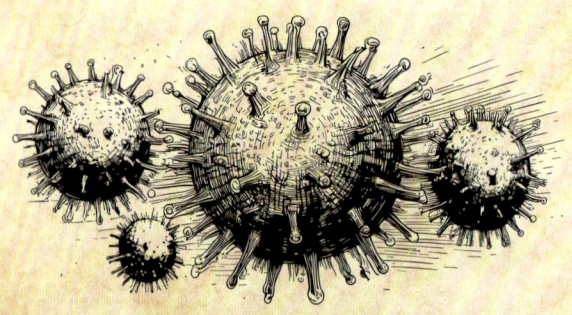

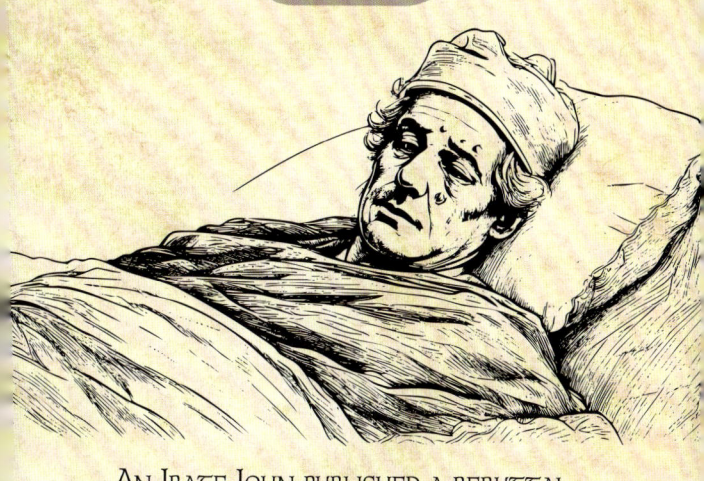

An Irate John published a rebuttal, calling the author a fraud.

On the night of John's supposed fever death, Jonathan published a message (again under a fake name), that John Partridge, a "cobbler, Starmonger and Quack", had passed away and admitted his fraudulent ways on his deathbed!

GEORGIAN GIGGLES

First published in 1739, Joe Miller's Jests could be bought for a single shilling, and his jokes became so well known that an overused joke became known as a 'Joe Miller'!

A FAMOUS TEACHER OF ARITHMETICK, WHO HAD LONG BEEN MARRIED WITHOUT BEING ABLE TO GET HIS WIFE WITH CHILD : ONE SAID TO HER, MADAM, YOUR HUSBAND IS AN EXCELLENT ARITHMETICIAN. YES, REPLIES SHE, ONLY HE CAN'T MULTIPLY.

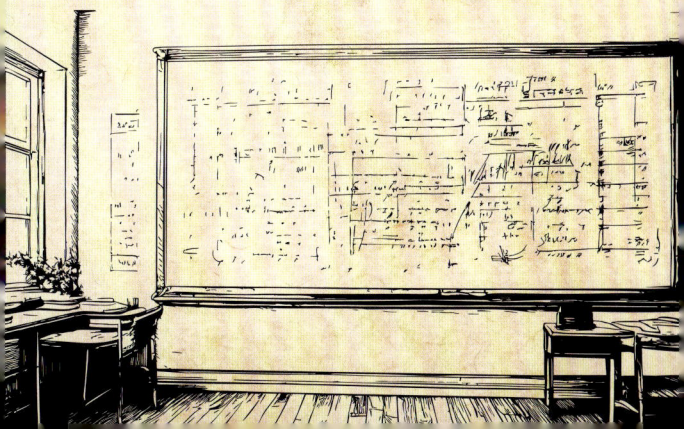

GEORGIAN GIGGLES

A COUNTRY FARMER GOING CROSS HIS GROUNDS IN THE DUSK OF THE EVENING, SPY'D A YOUNG FELLOW AND A LADY, VERY BUSY NEAR A FIVE BAR GATE, IN ONE OF HIS FIELDS, AND CALLING TO THEM TO KNOW WHAT THEY WERE ABOUT, SAID THE YOUNG MAN NO HARM, FARMER, WE ARE ONLY GOING TO PROP-A-GATE.

A LADY'S AGE HAPPENING TO BE QUESTIONED, SHE AFFIRMED SHE WAS BUT FORTY, AND CALL'D UPON A GENTLEMAN THAT WAS IN COMPANY FOR HIS OPINION; COUSIN, SAID SHE, DO YOU BELIEVE I AM IN THE RIGHT, WHEN I SAY I AM BUT FORTY? I OUGHT NOT TO DISPUTE IT, MADAM, REPLY'D HE, FOR I HAVE HEARD YOU SAY SO THESE TEN YEARS.

A BEGGAR ASKING ALMS UNDER THE NAME OF A POOR SCHOLAR, A GENTLEMAN TO WHOM HE APPLY'D HIMSELF, ASK'D HIM A QUESTION IN LATIN, THE FELLOW, SHAKING HIS HEAD, SAID HE DID NOT UNDERSTAND HIM: WHY, SAID THE GENTLEMAN, DID YOU NOT SAY YOU WERE A POOR SCHOLAR? YES, REPLY'D THE OTHER, A POOR ONE INDEED, SIRE, FOR I DON'T UNDERSTAND ONE WORD OF LATIN.

Did you know, April Fools Day dates back to the 1st April, 1700?

English pranksters wanted a day to play tricks on each other, and celebrate all things funny!

Next time you want to scare your gullible friends wth a fake spider, think about your ancestors who may have just done the same!

BOTTLED BANTER

In 1749, London newspapers advertised a show of a man who could fit his entire self into a wine bottle and sing a tune whilst inside, it also promised communication with the dead, and other 'impossible' tricks.

It was actually a bet between the Duke of Portland and the Earl of Chesterfield that caused this.

After discussing how gullible the public can be, the duke bet that he could gather a foolish paying audience for something evidently impossible... And he was right! Nearly every seat in the playhouse was filled - but no performer showed up! This caused riots within the audience, who began destroying the theater!

THIS PRANK STINKS
PART I

William Buckland, a paleontologist from the 19th century, believed that the way to grow a great lawn was by using bat guano. He spelled the word 'guano' in bat poop across one of the universities lawns.

PART 2

This was quickly removed, however the bat poop had already absorbed into the grass below, and within weeks, the universities lawn was growing brilliantly, but only in the word formation 'GUANO'!

VICTORIAN JOKES

Who knew the Victorians were such jokesters?

Why is a dog like a tree? Because they both lose their bark once they're dead.

VICTORIAN JOKES

Who is the greatest chicken-killer in Shakespeare?

Macbeth, because he did murder most foul.

IF WILLIAM PENN'S AUNTS KEPT A
PASTRY SHOP, WHAT WOULD BE THE
PRICES OF THEIR PIES?

THE PIE-RATES OF PENN'S AUNTS.

'WHY IS A MANUSCRIPT ALWAYS CALLED A **MS**? BECAUSE THAT IS THE STATE IN WHICH THE EDITOR FINDS IT.'

A LADY WROTE THE FOLLOWING LETTERS AT THE BOTTOM OF HER FLOUR BARREL:

OICURMT.

The Victorians loved a good prank, and it's no wonder why! It was so popular in fact, that even the newspapers of that time celebrated April Fools Day.

IN 1878, THE DAILY GRAPHIC, NEW YORK, FABRICATED THAT INVENTOR THOMAS EDISON HAD INVENTED A BRAND NEW MACHINE THAT COULD TRANSFORM WATER INTO WINE, AND SOIL INTO CEREAL! MANY NEWSPAPAERS REPRINTED THE STORY, NOT REALIZING THE FINEPRINT AT THE BOTTOM!

WILD WEST WIT

These entertaining jokes from
the Wild West are sure to make
you ye-ha-ha-haw!

WHILE PASSING A HOUSE ON THE ROAD, TWO VIRGINIA SALESMEN SPOTTED A VERY PECULIAR CHIMNEY, UNFINISHED, AND IT ATTRACTING THEIR ATTENTION, THEY ASKED A FLAXEN-HAIRED URCHIN STANDING NEAR THE HOUSE IF IT 'DRAWED WELL' WHEREUPON THE AFOREMENTIONED URCHIN GAVE THEM THE STINGING RETORT: 'YES, IT DRAWS ALL THE ATTENTION OF ALL THE D***** FOOLS THAT PASS THIS ROAD.'

A man said to a preacher, "That was an excellent sermon, but it was not original." The preacher was taken aback. The man said he had a book at home containing every word the preacher used. The next day the man brought the preacher a dictionary.

THERE WAS A MAN WHOSE LAST NAME WAS ROSE. AS A LARK, HE NAMED HIS DAUGHTER WILD, "WITH THE HAPPY CONCEIT OF HAVING HER CALLED WILD ROSE." BUT THAT SENTIMENT WAS "KNOCKED OUT" WHEN THE WOMAN GREW UP TO MARRY A MAN WHOSE LAST NAME WAS BULL.

Whatever troubles Adam had, No man could make him sore, By saying when he told a jest, "I've heard that joke before."

A fellow tells his ma that there are two holes in his trousers and then tells her that's where he puts his feet through.

A man got up one morning and couldn't find his alarm clock, so he asked his wife what had become of it. She said, "It went off at 6 o'clock."

In the 19th century, Palisade, Nevada was considered the most violent town in the US, a lawless town filled with bloodshed.

In reality, Palisade was peaceful, and crafted its poor image for the thrill of both residents and visitors alike, staging gunfights, hangings, and robberies, and became a must-see destination!

EDWARDIAN WIT

It's no secret that the turn of the century brought along even more humor, and the Edwardians LOVED it!

The following are just a few snippets from a comedian's collection in 1900.

Mrs Slybel: "That boy grows more like his father every day."

The Caller: "Poor dear. And have you tried everything?"

TRAMP: "MY PARD SAYS YE JIST GUV HIM SIXPENCE FOR HAVING ONE LEG."

B.NEVEOLENT: "YES, I DID."

TRAMP: "GIMME A SHILLING, WON'T YER? I'VE GOT TWO."

VISITOR: "So YOUR BROTHER IS TAKING LESSONS ON THE VIOLIN. IS HE MAKING PROGRESS?"

LITTLE GIRL: "YES'M; HE'S GOT SO NOW WE CAN TELL WHETHER HE IS TUNING OR PLAYING."

WORLD WAR FUN

In the First World War, the British took Ypres, and came across a damaged printing press. To pass the time, soldiers began printing their own satirical newspaper, The Wipers Times. Here are just two of the jokes found within their prints!

"Are you going over the top? If so be sure to first inspect our new line of velveteen corduroy plush breeches."

THREE TOMMIES SAT IN THE TRENCH
ONE DAY DISCUSSING THE WAR IN THE
NORMAL WAY, THEY TALK OF THE MUD,
THEY TALKED OF THE HUN, AND WHAT
WAS TO DO AND WHAT HAVE BEEN DONE,
THEY TALKED ABOUT RUM. BUT THE
POINT WHICH THEY ARGUED FROM POST
BACK TO PILLAR WAS WHETHER NOTTS
COUNTY COULD BEAT ASTON VILLA.

A 'bomb' was dropped over German troops on April 1st, in which the soldiers could be seen scrambling for cover.

After a while of waiting, they went to investigate the unexploded weapon, only to find it was a football with the words "April Fool!" and an anti-English quote.

ROARING TWENTIES

Found in a 1922 edition of the Daily News, New York - this timeless joke will have been read by many New Yorkers, and passed along to the next person who chooses to listen, no wonder this theme of joke is still popular today!

An american went into a London tea shop, took his seat and waited. Presently a bright-eyed waitress approached him and asked:

"Can I take your order?"
"Yes, two boiled eggs and a kind word."

THE WAITRESS BROUGHT THE EGGS AND WAS MOVING ON WHEN THE AMERICAN SAID:

"SAY! WHAT ABOUT THE KIND WORD?"

THE WAITRESS LEANED OVER AND WHISPERED:
"DON'T EAT THE EGGS."

WORLD BORE TWO

Everybody felt the impact of the Second
World War, and the way civillians chose to
fight the depression of the war was with
humor! Often making the opposing side
the butt of the joke!

WHY DO FRENCH TANKS HAVE REAR-VIEW MIRRORS? TO SEE THE BATTLEFIELD.

WHEN A SILVER AEROPLANE FLIES OVER, IT'S AMERICAN. WHEN THERE'S A GREEN 'PLANE, IT'S BRITISH. WHEN THERE ARE NO AIRCRAFT, THAT'S THE LUFTWAFFE.

General to private: "Have you come here to die?" Private to General: "No sir, I came here yester-die!"

A passenger train is fully loaded, and a German soldier, on leave, shares a compartment with a decrepit lady, a beautiful young French woman, and a young French man. The train enters a tunnel, and no one can see anything.

A kiss is heard, then a hollow slap. When the train comes out of the tunnel, the German has a horrible black eye.

So unlucky' thinks the German soldier. 'The French man gets the kiss and I get the blame!' 'Well done, my girl!' thinks the old lady. 'You stood up to that brute!'

The beautiful woman is puzzled. 'Why would that German kiss that old lady?'

The Frenchman, meanwhile, thinks 'How clever I am! I kiss the back of my hand, hit the German and no one suspects me!'

The Germans built a completely fake airfield to try and fool their enemies and waste their rescources, but unbeknownst to them they knew!

In retalliation the enemy planes flew over and bombed the airfield. When the Germans went to investigate, they found they had been fooled yet again! This time, fake wooden bombs with the inscription 'Wood for Wood' scattered the land!

"IS YOUR WIFE A BUTTERFLY?"
"SHE THINKS SHE IS, BUT THE WAY
SHE GOES THROUGH MY POCKETS SHE'S
MORE LIKE A MOTH."

FUN FORTIES

LITTLE BOY: "COULD I HAVE MY ARROW BACK? PLEASE? I SHOT IT INTO YOUR GARDEN."

NEIGHBOUR: "WHEREABOUTS IS IT?"

LITTLE BOY: "IN YOUR CAT."

She: "John, I hope I didn't see you smiling at that girl."

John: "I hope you didn't, my dear."

FIFTIES' FUNNIES

The 1950s brought along many new things. The best part wasn't the invention of the microwave oven though... No. It was the cheeky, hilarious punchlines!

There is a big moron and a little moron standing on a ledge, the big moron fell off, why didn't the little moron?

He was a little more on.